HALLIE
BENNETT

I0619587

BOOKS BY THIS AUTHOR

Standalones
Batter Up: An Instalove, Curvy Girl Romance
Wood Lessons: An Instalove, Curvy Girl Romance
Tees & Jeans Series
The Brother Bias: A Brother's Best Friend, Curvy Girl Romance
The Boss Bias: An Age Gap, Curvy Girl Romance
The Bad Boy Bias: An Opposites Attract, Curvy Girl Romance
Lumberjacks of High Ridge Series
Kept by the Beast: A Curvy Girl, Mountain Man Romance
Claimed by the Woodsman: A Surprise Pregnancy, Mountain Man Romance
Found by the Loner: A Curvy Girl, Mountain Man Romance
Christmas & Curves Series
Festive Fever: A Curvy Girl Holiday Romance
Curvy College Reunion Series
Campus Good Girl: A Curvy Girl/Jock Romance
Campus Queen: A Steamy Curvy Girl Romance
Campus Bookworm: A Shy Girl/Loner Guy Romance

For all the Hallmark fans who need a little more steam!

CHAPTER ONE

EMERY

I t's not every day you meet a movie star.

At least not for a girl like me.

But thanks to my friend Krista, this weekend I'll be surrounded by celebrities famous for their holiday movies at this year's MerryCon—a fun-filled convention for the Christmas-crazed, romantic movie lovers of the world.

Which includes me because I can't get enough of romance or Christmas.

Activity buzzes through the convention center as volunteers and vendors set up booths for the first day, holiday cheer ringing through the air. From my place in the volunteer line, I spy hundreds of snowflakes and ornaments hanging from the rafters while Christmas trees adorn the floor space. A winter wonderland meant to transport guests to the North Pole.

Enthusiasm pumps through my veins for the weekend to come, and I make a note to thank Krista again. As an early Christmas present, she'd signed me up to volunteer, hoping I'd get paired with my favorite actor: Calder Mayfield. Ever since he starred in my first Hallmark Christmas movie, I've been hooked—on him and the movies. A bevy of nerves flutters around my stomach at the possibility of meeting him.

Normally, I'm a practical kind of girl, understanding that the odds of matching with the man of my fictional dreams is as far-fetched as me managing to fit into size twelve jeans. But

Christmas is made for miracles, right? Magic and miracles. So where's the harm in a little dreaming?

Especially since I haven't had much luck meeting a man in real life for years. Unfortunately, the majority of my time these days is spent working from home—not much of a chance bumping into the love of my life there.

"Next." The woman at the check-in table motions me forward and asks for my name.

"Emery Michaels."

Searching through layers of lanyards covered in reindeer, she pulls one out with my name and hands it over. "You're in C13 with Thatcher North. Here's a packet of instructions and the itinerary for the weekend."

Butterflies of hope plummet in my stomach as disappointment takes their place. Not the best way to start MerryCon—having my dream of being paired with Calder dashed so soon. But I knew it was a longshot. At least I can still try to snag a meet and greet photo if I have free time.

Buoyed by the thought, I navigate my way towards C13. Arrows direct people to an area lined with booths, and mine's empty except for a plastic container stacked on a table with two chairs. A backdrop of red and white stripes hangs behind the table, promoting a candy cane theme. Charmed by the sight, I smile and break the seal on the welcome packet to read what's expected of me, the first sheet detailing how volunteers need to use the supplied holiday decorations to garnish the table. Seems easy enough.

Shrugging out of my cardigan before becoming a sweaty mess, I tug uncomfortably on my shirt, wishing Krista had chosen a men's tee instead of the women's when she'd filled out the volunteer form. This thin red fabric adheres to all the wrong places—emphasizing my roundness from breasts to hips. Attributes I've learned to flaunt to my advantage with the right clothing. But clingy tees are not it.

"Nothing for it now," I mumble, resigned to my fate, before unpacking the box of decor. Christmas trees intermingle with a hodgepodge of reindeer, Santas, and village items, all needing to be organized in some semblance of order. "This will be fun..."

While in work mode, my mind wanders to Thatcher North.

He's new to the made-for-TV romantic movies scene, but I've liked the two he's made—one for Hallmark and the other for the Hearts of America Channel or HAC.

Though a bit older than I prefer my leading men, he's still attractive with silver threading his dark hair and a beard shadowing his jaw. *Don't forget his eyes.* Whiskey-colored and just as warm, defined by heavy brows. A ripple of awareness assails me as I catalogue his handsome features.

Good grief! What are you thinking?

Shaking off the strange reaction, I resume the task of table decorating, burying any inappropriate musings. A notification from my phone pops up with Krista's name. "Hey, how's it going so far? Meet any hot actors yet?"

Snorting in amusement at the message, I type out what's happened so far, relaying the missed opportunity of being partnered with Calder.

"That's too bad," she sends with a frowny-face emoji. "But maybe you'll run into him while on break!"

Ever the optimist.

Though it's not far-fetched considering where we are. Bolstered by the possibility, a jaunty holiday tune hums in my throat. Who knows what the weekend has in store?

CHAPTER TWO

THATCHER

I regret my decision to attend MerryCon as soon as we drive under the welcome banner held by oversized nutcrackers, their air-filled bodies swaying in the winter breeze.

"Are you sure this is necessary?" I ask, a grim set to my mouth.

"Yes, you need this, and we're lucky someone else dropped out so you could take their spot. MerryCon is like the Super Bowl for people like you, Thatch. Where else can you meet super fans like these? Super fans who can petition to see you in more projects." My new manager, Leon, continues typing on his phone as he patiently answers the question I've asked multiple times before.

Unfortunately, he's right.

I need this weekend to boost my image and gain wider exposure to the fans of Hallmark, Lifetime, and HAC. But as more and more holiday decor fills my view along with the lines of people dressed in red and green, I contemplate how far I've fallen.

Growing up, I'd been one of the stars of a popular sitcom called *The Headley's*—used to red carpets and flashing lights—a far cry from this spectacle. Then the show ended, and I made poor decisions, choosing bad scripts until it became a chore finding someone willing to hire me as anything more than an extra.

Thankfully, my college degree came in handy for supplementing my income with remote coding work for various companies. It just wasn't my dream to sit behind a desk all day. I figured my acting career was over until an old buddy from the show reached out about a potential career reboot through movies popular on Hallmark and the like.

With his help and the hiring of Leon, it seemed things were back on track after booking two movies in one year. But I know as well as anyone how quickly that can change. Thus, MerryCon.

Be grateful they even want you.

Tension bunches in my shoulders at the reprisal. It's not that I have anything against a convention focused solely on the feel-good films, but what if no one recognizes me? What if a random exec sees me alone with no fans and decides the people don't want to see more of me on their screens? I'll be finished before really getting started... again.

Focus on the positive.

Like hanging out with George who played my younger brother on the show if we both manage to get free. Or celebrating my favorite holiday—Christmas—all weekend with loads of hot chocolate and cookies. An offhand chuckle escapes at what my personal trainer will think of that.

"What's so funny?"

"Nothing important." Eyeing the crowd outside, I confirm the day's schedule. "So, you said I'll be taking pictures at my booth before participating in the stocking decorating contest?"

"Yep. Then, tomorrow is the leading men's panel." Leon looks over at me as our driver parks at a back entrance. "But don't worry about forgetting anything. You'll have a volunteer assigned to help you, and I'm around if you need me. Keep in mind I'll be circulating behind the scenes for potential leads on roles, though, so try not to need me." He winks before getting out of the car, and I follow.

A volunteer helper. That sounds good. At least I'll have someone to talk to if no one lines up for a photo.

And someone to witness your failure.

CHAPTER THREE

EMERY

One of the coordinators does a final round of inspection before announcing they'll be allowing fans inside to line up. Nerves tingle at my fingertips as I double-check the directions for how to handle celebrity guests and MerryCon attendees.

Don't take unauthorized photos of celebrities.

Collect money from attendees before snapping their picture with the celebrity.

Common sense stuff.

Expelling a determined breath, I wait next to the sign denoting Thatcher North's booth and watch as crowds of mostly women hustle into the long rectangular area. Soon queues form on either side of me for Macy Adams and Chris Horn, but nothing yet for Thatcher.

It's okay. It's still early.

Twenty minutes pass with no change, then an exuberant cry sweeps over the congregated masses as a set of double doors opens to reveal the group of celebrities participating for the weekend. Flashes brighten the room, despite the repeated warnings posted on flyers and from roving volunteers that unauthorized photography is prohibited.

Rising to my tiptoes to glimpse a familiar face, a spurt of energy lifts me higher, but it's too difficult to identify anyone from so far away.

The actors disperse to their assigned booths after a couple of group photos and eager chatter erupts. My gaze tracks the movement in front of me until Thatcher's tall form appears. Purposeful steps set him apart from the leisurely pace of those around him—along with the strained expression tightening his face.

When he's close enough to hear me over the crowd, I offer a hand for him to shake and smile in greeting, hoping to put him at ease. "Hi, I'm Emery, your volunteer for the weekend. Nice to meet you."

His hand jerks in mine, brows furrowing, before replying. "Thatcher, but some call me Thatch."

"Looks like this will be our home for the next four days. Are you ready to meet all of your adoring fans?" I tease as we take our seats behind the table. A conspicuous emptiness lies in front of us compared to the bulging rows of people around the room.

He snorts in disbelief. "Adoring might be pushing it. Fans might be too much, as well." The garland-covered poles serving as line boundaries loom—perfect and untouched—as if confirming his suspicions.

"I wouldn't worry too much. People will come. *Christmas Downtown* and *Spring Forward* were cute, so I'm sure you'll have lots of fans."

"You've seen my movies?"

Leaning to the side to face him more fully, I nod. "Of course! I watch a ton of these movies, but your Christmas one was actually really sweet. I liked how your character opened up towards the end and was willing to be vulnerable in order to get the girl." The movie also cemented a phenomenon I coined as "The North Effect": a moment in a previously boring movie when the leading man does or says something that suddenly shows him in a whole new light—upping the film's entertainment and the man's attractiveness factor.

It's kind of funny that MerryCon paired us together when I consider the phenomenon. And how I've only seen two of his films compared to the multitude of Calder Mayfield's, yet I've never once created a "Mayfield Effect".

Just remember: it only works on fictional characters. It's not real.

"Thank you. It's nice to hear a positive review." A note of defeat inches into his voice, and my defenses rise. I've heard enough bashing on my taste in movies that I'm always prepared to offer an opposition.

"Have there been negative reviews? Aside from the usual haters who like to trash romance?" If there was one thing that pissed me off, it was people judging Hallmark or Lifetime movies harshly for "repeated" or "unrealistic" storylines when the same could be said for a number of genres. Why people can't be left to love what they love without reprisal is beyond me.

"None that I know of... I was speaking more from past experiences." Before I can question him further, a trio of women approach for pictures. Dropping the conversation, I take each woman's phone to snap their photos, focusing on what I'm here for—mediating the meet and greets instead of prying into Thatcher's personal life.

No matter how intriguing it may be...

CHAPTER FOUR

THATCHER

C*ontrol yourself. You're in public.*

I chastise my body for responding to Emery as another woman wraps an arm around my waist for her picture. All I need is a visible hard-on etched permanently in these women's photo albums. That won't be good for the wholesome image I need to project in keeping with Hallmark and HAC. Lifetime allows more leeway as far as their stars' actions, however, my erection probably pushes the boundaries. Not to mention it's inappropriate as hell.

But damn. Emery is a lush beauty who smells like snickerdoodles—my favorite cookie. And all I want to do is take a bite. *Or two. Or three.*

"Thank you for doing this! I just loved you in *The Headley's*." The mention of my old show surprises me, and my cursory polite expression morphs into a genuine one of gratefulness.

"I appreciate your support. That show changed my life, so it's great when people share their love of a pivotal project and role for me." After giving her a hug as farewell, Emery guides another lady to me, and my mind reverts back to its former musings. *Forbidden* former musings.

Emery's my volunteer and too young for the likes of me. Nothing good can come of this attraction. Yet, I can't help the spike of lust shooting through my cock as she adjusts her position for a better camera angle. Generous breasts push against

13

the limits of her tee along with a soft, curved stomach I imagine running my tongue over before delving lower and tasting...

Fuck! Stop thinking about it. About her.

Once the short line for pictures finally disappears, we stand awkwardly, waiting for more people. Attempting to distract myself, I ask, "Who are you excited to see this weekend? I assume you volunteered because you've got some fan crushes."

An endearing blush leaps to her cheeks, and an unexpected wave of jealousy crashes into my stomach. What man is she imagining? Who's her type?

"Well, my friend sent in the volunteer form as a Christmas gift, since she knows how much I love these movies. But yes, there are a couple of people I wouldn't mind meeting."

"Like?" I press, determined to learn their names. *Like it has any bearing on me. I'm sure as hell not one of them.*

"I'm not sure I should say..."

"Don't worry about hurting my feelings or that I'll share. Most of these people are strangers to me, too." The majority of the cast I've worked with were also newbies to the channels and weren't participating in this year's MerryCon. Aside from George, the Hallmark, Lifetime, and HAC stars were complete unknowns.

She toys with one of the reindeer decorating the table, flipping it over and over, before responding. "Marsha Kent is one of my favorites along with Patrick Lorne. But the top person on my wishlist to meet is Calder Mayfield. He was in the first HAC Christmas film I watched, so he's always someone I look forward to seeing."

Calder Mayfield. No surprise there. An image of the handsome young man flashes in my mind as my attention snaps to his booth across the way. Hoards of fans fill his line, wrapping like a snake around one of the Christmas trees standing tall in the middle of the space. There's even a volunteer dedicated to directing more fans into an orderly fashion, so the rest of the crowd isn't blocked from getting to neighboring booths.

"I don't know any of them personally, but I've heard good things. Seems like the networks really like them." Calder alone released six films this year, a sum that incited my envy.

If only I could inspire such a degree of confidence in network execs, directors, fans...

"I'm glad to hear none of them are secretly horrible people." Emery chuckles, green eyes crinkling at the corners in humor, and the breath freezes in my lungs in reaction. Immediately, I want to make her laugh again, to drift in the musical sound of her happiness.

Was that dialogue in one of your scripts? I'm usually not a very flowery thinker when it comes to women—my thoughts keep routinely to the dirt: straightforward and filthy.

Another couple of hours pass with people visiting at various times, leaving us alone to chat about things outside of MerryCon, a fact that should depress but instead pleases me. If it weren't for Emery, there would be more disappointment at having so few fans, evidence that my earlier fear of failure is proving true. But she lifts my spirits with tales of her personal life—feeding my irrational desire to learn more about her—and somehow it overshadows the lack of fans.

"Mr. North, are you ready for the stocking decorating contest? We're gathering contestants now." A man with a clipboard interrupts, beckoning us to follow him, and Emery puts out a "Be right back" sign before tagging along beside me.

Weaving through the chattering crowd is a chore as our escort hurries forward. Instinctively, my hand reaches for Emery's to lead her along an easier path while I wade through stationary groups of people.

Her palm is soft, warm, and I gently squeeze, relishing the feel of her hand in mine. Like it belongs there. Like it's right. And an unsettling sensation takes root near my heart at how strong of a pull she has on me after only a few hours.

"You'll be seated across from Mr. Mayfield." The man leading us gestures to two empty chairs. "Everything you need is already on the table, and I'll be back to check on everyone in an hour when we have the judging. Have fun!"

Pulling a seat out for Emery, my hands clench on the backrest at her blatant interest in our tablemate—the man at the top of her wishlist. A sharp pain radiates in my jaw, and I make a conscious effort to relax. It's stupid to get worked up over a woman I barely know. A stranger. But I want her pretty eyes on me, not Calder fucking Mayfield.

Settle down. It's not like she belongs to you... yet.

CHAPTER FIVE

EMERY

"Welcome to our little crafting wonderland! I hope you have a clue about how to do this, since I'm at a loss." Calder's charming grin disarms my calm composure, and a silent prayer of thanks flies up to the heavens at my good fortune. We may not have been paired together but sitting with him while decorating stockings works, too.

"Didn't you learn anything from all your Christmas movies?" I flirt, taking the seat Thatcher offers and noticing a slight frown on his face, before turning back to Calder. "By now, you should be an expert at holiday tasks: decorating, baking, caroling..."

"None of it's stuck with me, I'm afraid. Probably because it helps to have a partner during such things." He winks at me as a scoffing huff comes from Thatcher.

Twisting to the right, irritated waves roll off him, surprising me with their intensity, and the change from affable guy to this is baffling. "You disagree?"

He brushes over the question with a noncommittal shake of his head and grabs a blank red stocking from the pile stacked at the center of the table. Dumping it in front of me, he picks up another one before selecting white puff paint. "We should get started. Do you know what you're putting on yours?"

I'm tempted to continue the previous conversation, but Calder's volunteer appears, distracting him. Deflating at the abrupt halt of our banter, I comfort myself with the knowledge that I didn't make a complete fool of myself and actually held a fun, teasing conversation. Krista will be so proud.

You did the same thing with Thatcher, too.

"You're humming that song again. Joy to the World, right?"

Thankful for the intrusion—halting the bewildered spiral my mind was heading down with Thatcher and Calder—I dip my head in affirmation. "Yeah, it's my favorite Christmas song, but what do you mean by again?"

"Earlier while taking photos, you hummed it then, too." Astonishment jolts through my veins at the keen observation. I'm not used to someone noticing such small details about me, and it's unnerving but pleasant. What else has he noticed?

"Oh," I say stupidly, bringing a hot glue gun closer to add a tiny poinsettia to my stocking. "Sorry if it annoys you; I'll try to keep the holiday songs to a minimum. I know a lot of people don't care for Christmas music."

"It's not annoying... It's comforting. Like snowfall on Christmas Eve, lights twinkling in the window, steam rising from hot mugs of cocoa." The words delivered in his low tone curl around me—enticing and intimate—as if we weren't in the middle of a convention center, and instead, cabin walls cocooned us in warmth during a cold winter's night.

Quit dreaming.

A waft of heat trembles over my skin, and our eyes connect until a burn scorches my fingers, eliciting a yelp of pain. Relinquishing the hot glue gun in a burst of shock, I move to peel the molten globs of glue off my fingertips, but Thatcher catches my hand to do it himself.

"Damn, are you okay? *Fuck!*" He jerks back from the sting of glue, tossing the offending clump aside, and I can't resist a soft snicker at his reaction.

"I don't think you're supposed to curse at MerryCon. It's supposed to be family-friendly."

"Yeah, well, they should've thought of that before providing these dangerous little suckers." His lips purse to blow a cool stream of air over the smarting tips of my fingers, the tender gesture having the opposite effect on my hormones, revving them up in response to such an intimate act.

The North Effect.

It's real.

With one kind deed, my perception of Thatcher shifts. His breath on my skin. His murmured description of a romantic evening. Even his scent engulfs me in a swift bombardment of need. And here I am, lecturing him on being appropriate at a family event.

What's wrong with me?

Not five minutes ago, I was excited to flirt with Calder Mayfield—my longtime tv crush—but now I'm a mess of hormones for Thatcher North? A completely off-limits man who's at least ten years my senior and is just being courteous? Not flirtatious or interested in anything beyond a professional acquaintance. After Sunday, he'll be gone, and I'll still be here.

"Does that feel better?" he asks, glancing up to gauge my pain level.

"It's fine." Extracting my hand from his, I rub it on my thigh in an effort to calm down. "I'll be more careful going forward, though I don't know why I need to make one. They won't be judging my stocking. All they care about is yours."

"You're doing it for fun, so your MerryCon weekend isn't spent performing tedious tasks like being the designated photographer. Plus, if yours turns out better, I'm stealing it for a better chance at winning." The devilish gleam in his brown eyes dares me to play along, and it's impossible for me to resist.

"Ah, so your devious plan finally comes to light. Unfortunately, I don't condone cheating." My shoulders shrug in nonchalance while my lips wobble in an effort to avoid smiling.

"It's not cheating if we're a team. Isn't there some way to tempt you to my side?" Thatcher's voice deepens, a lone finger stroking the back of my hand as golden sparks of humor intersperse with the amber color of his eyes. When did he get so close?

Swallowing past the lump clogging my throat, I open my mouth to reply when Calder cuts in, like a beacon trying to break through the fog I've found myself floating in. "Give it up, Thatch. No matter what you do, it's obvious I'll be the winner." His outrageous statement lightens the mood, shattering our private moment, providing momentary relief from my heightened awareness of Thatcher.

"We'll see..." An underlying current runs beneath Thatcher's statement. One that sounds more serious than a crafting contest warrants, and the silly part of me wonders if it's jealousy due to my gushing over Calder earlier.

Get real. We're not in high school. Or a movie.

CHAPTER SIX

THATCHER

After Calder interrupts, we stick to small talk, finishing the stockings, and seeking to outdo the other in a game of "Anything You Can Do, I Can Do Better". I've never laughed so much in my life or had such fun. Growing up on set, we weren't allowed much time off, and my family wasn't the type featured in most of the Hallmark movies. We didn't have holiday traditions. We weren't close.

Hell, this was my first time having a stocking, and it wasn't even technically mine. It's not like I'd take this ugly thing home to hang on my mantel. But Emery sparkled with Christmas spirit, eager to aid me when she wasn't trying to beat me. She made a simple act exhilarating. Elevated it to a meaningful bonding moment instead of a necessary ploy for good PR at MerryCon.

"I'm not sure your stocking can take much more. You've drowned it in so many snowmen and ornaments, I'm surprised the felt hasn't torn yet. Less is more, you know." Emery giggles, an adorable release I yearn to capture with my mouth. To breathe her in and seize some of that joy for myself.

"*More* is more," I counter. "You can never have too much Christmas."

"Didn't you say that in *Christmas Downtown*?"

"Maybe... Doesn't mean it's not true, though." She laughs again at my rejoinder, and adrenaline explodes in my veins as if

21

I'm a thrillseeker coming off the high of a skydive or racing a car at two hundred miles per hour.

God, I'm obsessed. And in serious fucking trouble.

We can't get involved. Forget about age differences or our professional relationship. I need to focus on my career, on staying the course and not messing things up the second time around. Which doesn't leave much time for a relationship—assuming she's interested.

Don't forget about her crush on Calder.

Logically, I know nothing will come of it: Calder could be seeing someone and Emery's feelings are based on a fictional character—not a real person. But that doesn't discount the fact that he's closer to her age and more successful than me.

"If I can have all of the celebrity participants line up over here, please! We'll bring everyone onstage for the judging." The coordinator from earlier stands towards the front of the room, waving for us to join him. "Volunteers stay behind to help clean up the tables. You will meet your celebrity back at your booths after the contest has ended. Thank you everyone!"

"Guess that's my cue."

"Good luck! I'll see you afterwards." Emery crosses her fingers before shooing me away. Reluctant to leave her, I shuffle forward, chastising my stupidity. It's not like she's going anywhere. Besides, this weekend is about connecting with people and gaining a wider fanbase. I can't do that by focusing on one woman instead of partaking in MerryCon activities like this contest.

Resolve stiffens my spine as I walk onstage with a good-humored smile for the cheering crowd and journalists covering the event. I can do this. It's my sole purpose for being here.

Thankfully, the contest host is hilarious and talented at keeping an efficient pace. Forty-five minutes flash by in a whirlwind of laughter and good-natured ribbing as each celebrity's stocking is inspected. And while I don't place in the top three, the lively atmosphere bursting with happy chatter helps me understand why people love these holiday films so much.

There's a wholesome sweetness to a Christmas romance that guarantees a happily ever after. A quality that circumvents cynical attitudes held during the rest of the year. And it's not fake. As I absorb the numerous sounds and sights, a new respect for the season and these fans grows. These people are genuine and loyal. Why else would some travel thousands of miles to meet their favorite small-screen star?

The people I've worked with also shared those personality traits, and though I appreciated it, it never sunk in how rare that can be in this industry—even with my past terrible luck. Strolling back to my booth after completing a round of photos and autographs, it occurs to me that part of Emery's draw is her authentic, kind self. Sure, her curves are sexy as hell, but it's those inner qualities that shine through the most. She exudes the Hallmark ideals more than anyone I've ever met.

And she's snared me in a web made of those infinitesimal strands.

Upon returning to the booth, I half-heartedly wonder how to escape those bounds when most of me just wants to kiss her pink-glossed lips until they're red and swollen, gasping my name in a room hidden away from a mass of onlookers. Maybe she'll say something abhorrent. Treat a fan rudely. Then my fantasy of her can disappear like the sun on a stormy day.

However, as morning fades to afternoon, she remains perfect: friendly and patient with anyone who stops for a one-on-one with me. And by the end of the day, I'm no closer to shutting her out of my head or heart. And my cock... A fucking steel rod I attempt to hide.

"The volunteer packet said to leave everything as-is for tomorrow, so I think we're good to go for the night." Emery snatches the cardigan she'd left off for most of the day from the back of her chair and tugs it on, causing her breasts to strain the flimsy tee. "Is there anything else you need from me?"

You mean like your pretty mouth on mine? Your delicate nails scratching my back? Your thick thighs wrapped around my waist?

Ignoring the train of illicit thoughts, I ask for something simpler and, hopefully, less demanding. "Can I get your number? I meant to ask earlier but got caught up in the day. It might be good for us to have a way to contact each other if we ever get separated this weekend."

"Sure, you're totally right."

We've just finished exchanging numbers when Leon intrudes. Jacket wrinkled and hair askew, he looks like he's had a busy day. Let's hope it bodes well for me considering how unfocused I've been today.

"Hey, Thatch, are you ready to hit the road?"

"Yeah, we're done here." Zipping up my coat, I turn towards Emery. "Guess I'll see you tomorrow. Have a good night and drive safely." Her expression softens, a sweet flush pinkening her cheeks before returning the farewell and leaving.

Leon offers a rundown of his day as we step outside, but it dulls to a distant buzzing, my mind still with Emery, imagining walking her to her car, going home with her. Spending the night exploring the hills and valleys of her body until we both fall asleep exhausted, curled around each other.

What a perfect evening that would be.

CHAPTER SEVEN

EMERY

A frigid wind scrapes across my skin as I hurry across the parking lot and into the convention building before day two of MerryCon starts. There's a marked change to my emotions today versus yesterday. The most noticeable? The jumble of knots that's taken residence in my belly.

And it's all Thatcher North's fault.

Last night, he texted me twice—first, to make sure I made it home okay, and second, to ask what kind of drink I'd like in the morning. Both were thoughtful inquiries. Both built romantic scenarios where a normal girl like me interests the handsome and mature movie actor, especially when our second conversation deviated into personal territory.

Fanciful tales of our whirlwind romance kept me up half the night until my sleep-deprived brain cooked up a plan of seduction. Or rather, a test to gauge his interest. The specifics were hazy, but the first step included me wearing a sheer lace bra instead of the sturdier one from yesterday. A bra designed to showcase my nipples through the ultra-fine tee shirt I'm wearing.

I brought another cardigan to cover up when needed—after all, this is supposed to be family-appropriate—otherwise, I'll stay exposed and open to Thatcher's gaze. Ready to discover whether curious desire or impassivity lived in his eyes at the sight of my outlined body.

Or disgust. You're forgetting another key choice.

That disheartening thought gets shoved down deep because if I overthink this, begin cataloguing every roll and flaw, I'll lose my nerve.

I'm not usually so forward, but we're crunched for time. The weekend will be over soon, my opportunity lost. Besides, Krista's enthusiastic texts encouraged me to act wildly and emboldened me when my confidence flailed. She'd pestered me with questions yesterday, wondering how my day went, and when she'd found out about my unexpected reaction to Thatcher? Her scream of delight arced through the phone and pierced my eardrum.

So, she was definitely onboard with my bold scheme.

"Hey, this is for you." Thatcher arrives with hands full of two coffees—one hot and one cold—and I'm grateful to see him because there's no turning back now. "Though, I'm not sure how you can drink a freezing cold coffee in this kind of weather."

"It's good all year-round, trust me. Plus, I hate waiting for hot coffee to cool down; it's an odd quirk." Sipping the hazelnut-flavored drink, I hum in pleasure at the sugary refreshment.

"Hell, if it causes you to make that sound again, I don't care if it's twenty below outside. I'll get it whenever you want." A flare of heat ignites in his eyes, and a tremulous smile of encouragement forms on my mouth.

Maybe there's no need for a test if he's going to say things like that. Maybe this will be easier that I thought.

"Promise?"

"Cross my heart." He draws an X over his chest before leaning closer. "Should we seal it with a handshake? A kiss?"

Definitely don't need a test.

"Not here. Not now. I'll just have to trust you." People mill about the arena, traipsing from line to line, and I can only imagine what their reaction would be to a kiss between one of the actors and his volunteer. Mayhem would ensue. And I don't want gossip or bad publicity circulating about Thatcher.

He told me yesterday during our downtime about the purpose of this weekend. How he messed up his career with youthful mistakes and was trying to resurrect it with a strategic PR plan created by his manager. An important point was having a successful MerryCon experience.

Kissing me in public? That would only overshadow any progress he made.

A compassionate expression crinkles the corners of his eyes and mouth. "You can trust me, sweetheart. Never fear." The endearment melts the last of my doubts about his feelings towards me. This may not be a forever kind of affair—and I'm not the type of woman who goes for flings—but I'm willing to take the leap, to explore whatever is developing between us.

"Good morning! Mr. North, you're part of the first panel today: Leading Men Leading Christmas. Just come with me, so we can prepare you for your entrance." A woman named Mandy, based on her lanyard ID, reminds me we're not alone as we shuffle through the crowd. For the second time in two days, Thatcher and I have been interrupted during an intense emotional moment, and I prevent a bubble of laughter from escaping. How ironic that our lives are emulating one of the iconic scenes from these holiday movies: the almost kiss.

When we arrive backstage, Mandy explains how each actor will come out at different intervals until everyone's introduced. "You're third on the roster, so you have about a fifteen minute wait before being called. You can hang out here if you want or take a seat over there." She points to a round of chairs occupied by other stars I recognize, each playing on their phone.

While Thatcher finishes with Mandy, I creep nearer to the black curtain separating us from the rest of the stage, peeking out the side only to be blinded by lights. Jerking back, my body slams into a hard chest, heat emanating from Thatcher—his cologne identifying him immediately. Large hands cup my arms before sliding higher to massage my shoulders.

"Careful, sweetheart. Wouldn't want you to fall." The whispered warning slips through tendrils of hair, warming my ear. A furor of emotions bursts to life.

This is what I want.

This is what I need.

So, I lean into his embrace, pining for Christmas magic.

CHAPTER EIGHT

THATCHER

Emery's acceptance of my touch goes a long way towards allaying my worries of continuing this connection between us. Yesterday after MerryCon, I tried listing all the obstacles in our way—why this was a terrible idea. And every time my mind rationalized its way out.

It'll just be a fling. No harm, no foul.

She won't be interested. Problem solved.

Then this morning that lightning bolt of attraction I felt when I first met her magnified into a fucking supernova, and staying away became impossible. For better or worse, we're going to see this through.

Mahogany curls tangle with my beard before I gather her hair over one shoulder, drifting my mouth over the back of her exposed neck, almost tasting the brown sugar and cinnamon scent rising from her heated skin. *Delicious.* Tempted beyond reason—deciding to escalate our bond before time runs out—my tongue steals a quick sample of the flavor. "Damn, you really are a Christmas treat, aren't you? All sugar and spice. Tell me, sweetheart, when I lick between your thighs, will you be more spicy or sweet?"

"You'll have to... find out... for yourself," she stutters as my fingers trace the raised tip of one breast before gently pinching it. The thrill of her easy acceptance makes me dizzy. Head tilting back, Emery's throaty gasp rouses my cock to an agitated state, aching behind the confines of my jeans.

"Shhh... sweet girl. We can't be caught like this. Wet cream spreading along your pussy lips. Nipples budding to hard points. Did you think I wouldn't notice?" I nip her ear in retribution for the torment of her breasts butting against thin fabric, instinctively understanding she'd wanted to tease me, a stark contrast to yesterday when she'd kept completely covered. "And my visible arousal shocking the poor, innocent mothers and grandmothers out in the crowd. Is that what you want? To be caught?"

"No... I'll be quiet," she vows, a brave hand reaching back to brush against my erection. A pulse of need centers on her touch. Man, I wish we were alone. Wish she lay beneath me, naked and writhing, calling my name over and over...

"Our next guest is Thatcher North! Everyone welcome him to the stage!" The booming voice pounds in my head, and Emery straightens, pulling the sides of her cardigan together to hide her arousal.

Whipping around, eyes wide in alarm, she coaxes me towards the stage as my name's repeated. "Go! He's calling for you." Her gaze drops down, and a worried frown replaces the look of lust she wore earlier.

"It can't be helped now," I mumble, adjusting the clear bulge along my thigh. "Hopefully, people are too distracted to notice."

"Seems he's a little shy... Thatcher North, come on out! We don't bite!" The crowd howls in amusement, and I hustle to join the panel. Autopilot settles over me as question after question is asked.

What's my favorite Christmas movie? Who would I like to work with?

All rote answers that Leon and I worked on prior to arriving at MerryCon. But the fans don't seem to notice I'm not fully present—stuck backstage where a gorgeous brunette waits for me. I don't know how I'm going to get through the rest of the day with her by my side and not touch her the way I want. To keep things suitable for the public.

As it turns out, it's even more difficult than I expected.

After the panel, Emery and I retreat to our booth where a meager number of people approach the table for photos—once again allowing us to freely talk and giving me a reason to be happy for the lack of fans. Leon won't be pleased, but I couldn't care less at this point. We'd work on it in the new year.

Time moves quickly as I slide deeper under Emery's spell, completely immersed in my need to have her for my own, and when the clock finally ticks towards the day's end, I risk pressing for more. "Would you like to have dinner with me? We could go out or grab something and go to my hotel or your home. It's up to you. I just don't want to let you go yet."

"How about pizza at my place?" she offers, and I promptly agree, texting Leon to leave without me. He assumes I'm hanging out with George, but I don't correct him. Emery's place in my life will become clear soon enough, if tonight goes well. Best to wait and apprise him of the situation once we have a better understanding of it ourselves.

We sit in her living room two hours later, polishing off the last bite of cinnamon twists we ordered for dessert while an HAC movie plays on the tv. "Haven't had enough yet?" I ask, amused by her dedication to these films.

"Nope." She shakes her head vehemently before licking a drop of icing from her thumb. "This is my favorite time of year for movies because I love them all. No matter how corny."

Distracted by the move, I snatch her hand and bring it to my mouth, sucking on the damp spot left behind at the tip. "You're a hopeless romantic, aren't you?" I murmur, nibbling along her fingertips, savoring the slight give of her flesh to my roving teeth.

"Mmm... I prefer hopeful rather than hopeless."

"I like that. *Hopeful*... Such a pretty girl hoping for love." She shivers as I forge a path of kisses along her palm, pausing at her wrist to nuzzle the erratic pulse beating behind such fragile skin, then continuing upward until my mouth hovers over hers. "Will you let me kiss you, sweetheart?"

"Please. It's what I've been craving all day."

The confession demolishes what's left of my control, and with a groan of desperation, I eliminate the inch of space between us. Emery sinks into the overstuffed couch as my lips and teeth devour her like a hungering wolf. Sweet bursts of sugar coax me further as our tongues entwine, and a sense of rightness burns in my chest.

It's unexplainable. Irrational.

Yet, this feels like my last first kiss. Like I've found the woman who's meant to be mine.

Finally.

Frenzied hands search under her shirt before finding the plump curves of her breasts, barely shielded by the feeble barrier of a lace bra. "Take it off," she begs, arching higher to give me access to the clips at the back. "Take it all off."

"Are you sure?" A paltry amount of restraint remains in my body, but I want Emery to be absolutely certain this is what she wants. "We can stop here. There's more than enough of you to enjoy as-is."

"No." She cups my cheek, nails lightly grazing my beard, blue eyes clear and resolute. "We've known each other for less than forty-eight hours, but I don't care. I need your body blanketing mine, skin to skin. Want to feel every part of you surrounding me, inside me."

Lust and affection knit together at the admission—spoken as if pulled from the depths of my own desire—and I can't deny her.

"I'm yours, sweetheart. Here to satisfy your every wish."

CHAPTER NINE

Thatcher's words resound in my head.

I'm yours.

Here to satisfy your every wish.

My Christmas dream has come to life as if I lived in the steamy version of a Hallmark movie. Where I can revel in his passionate touch instead of fading to black, never knowing the pleasure he could give me.

Unsteadily, we stumble towards my room with me leading the way while he drags our clothes off, my bumbling hands just getting in the way. When we tumble onto my bed, all that remains is my skimpy panties and his jeans, something I stretch to rectify, but he swats my hand aside.

"Not yet, sweetheart. Just lay back and let me soak in the vision of you naked and needy for me."

My body freezes in place as a seed of insecurity prods the bubble of confidence encompassing me. In this position, on my back, the extra pounds around my waist spread into a doughy blob while my breasts flatten outward—not the most flattering pose.

It's not like he's a virgin. He's seen a woman nude before.

But one as chubby as me?

Past lovers never complained, but they also never praised me either. Comments usually focused on how excited and impatient they were to fuck instead of devoting time to complimenting me. Looking back, that should've been my first clue to avoid sleeping with them, especially considering how all of them ended up passing out after finishing—but before I did.

"Fuck, you're the sexiest little Christmas gift I've ever gotten. All curves and glowing, soft skin. You shouldn't ever cover up. I need to be able to kiss and touch you whenever I want—no barriers."

My lungs struggle for breath. Clearly, my fear is unwarranted, but I can't resist fishing for more confirmation. Thatcher is older, more experienced, and while the silver in his hair lends an air of sophistication, it also denotes years probably spent with beautiful actresses, a stark contrast to me. "You don't think there's... too much of me?"

"Are you kidding? You're perfect as you are." A ferocity enters his expression, eliciting a quiver of yearning that intensifies in my heart—and my core as wetness coats the tender flesh. "Let anyone say something different, and they'll quickly see their error."

Thatcher bends to cage me against the bed, skimming a kiss over my belly button while removing my panties. "Trust me to protect you from any of the naysayers. Trust me to give you only pleasure. Trust me to love..." His words are buried between my thighs, his bearded jaw nudging my legs apart before rasping over sensitive nerve endings. The electrifying swipe of his tongue wrests a startled exclamation from my lips—nobody's ever gone down on me before.

Which might explain the lack of orgasms from those men.

Fresh insight awakens a clawing demand for more, to finally experience what my friends have, to learn what it's like to have a considerate lover. "Don't stop. Please, don't stop." I latch onto his wavy hair, urging him closer, pleading for him to hurry.

"What did I say, sweetheart?" He blows a teasing waft of air over my clit before sucking one swollen pussy lip into the heat of his mouth. "*Trust me*. I don't plan on leaving until I've drunk my fill of this dripping cunt. And even then, it's debatable because you're fucking spicy, sweetheart. Cinnamon-hot like my favorite holiday treat. And so, so good for me... So delicious."

I'm left speechless, unintelligible sounds of ecstasy pervading the room as my hips buck underneath him, skeins of hair sticking to the sweat on my face. How he can have me close to the brink so soon is beyond me and a testament to his skill. Muscles tense and release, frantic for relief. Nerves tingle, on the precipice of detonating into a millions sparks of pleasure.

Greedy grunts of satisfaction emerge from Thatcher—primitive and arousing, unearthing a previously unknown part of me eager to please, to submit to his command. A feministic portion of my brain balks at the idea until I rationalize that it's only in bed. When we make love, he can ask whatever he wants from me because I *do* trust him. Already he's surpassed any other man I've been with, it's obvious my emotions and pleasure matter to him. And that makes all the difference.

"Thatcher..."

Two fingers delve deeper, searching, before finding a roughened spot inside me and rubbing intently. *Oh my god*. The combination of his mouth's steady suction on my clit and rough pads stroking my G-spot culminates in a blazing orgasm—tremors of euphoria blocking out everything except for Thatcher's continued gentled ministrations as my entire body bows in gratification.

Eventually, he traces a lazy path up my glistening skin, nipping and laving spots he finds of interest, leaving his fingers to linger below in a slow rhythm. "How are you doing, sweetheart?"

"Good... great..." Coherent sentences fail me as I try to catch my breath. "You've got quite a mouth on you." At his smirk, I hurry to explain, embarrassed. "I mean a dirty mouth... It was surprising considering how your roles on tv aren't quite as explicit."

"That's why it's called acting. Plus, I keep it PG in professional environments, but with you?" His palm suddenly slams hard against my engorged clit as a wicked glint shadows his expression. "I lose control, and all I want to do is whisper every filthy fantasy I have about you."

I like the sound of that. A lot.

"And what are you fantasizing about now?"

CHAPTER TEN

THATCHER

I remove drenched fingers and paint each of her nipples with the dew from her pussy, transfixed by the shining peaks. "You really want to know?"

Emery nods, licking her lips in sensual curiosity, body undulating beneath mine. *God, she's beautiful.* Whether decked out in MerryCon gear or wearing nothing but a flush of contentment, she's the most exquisite woman I've ever seen. A curvy little Christmas present. And she belongs to me.

"Fucking you from behind while you play with your tits. I want to watch them bounce and redden as they overflow your delicate hands. It's only fair to see them in all their glory after your teasing today." My head dips to suck the cream from her nipples, loving the taste of salt and sugar.

"Is that all?" she asks, attempting a tone of nonchalance but her heightened breathing and racing pulse belies a calm attitude.

"Well, I forewent the nipple clamps, watching the chain connecting them weigh on your breasts, making the tips so sensitive that a touch of your finger brings you to the edge." An image we'll reenact at a later date if I have anything to say about it. "But I thought it might be too much too soon. I need to ease you into my kind of loving, sweetheart."

A kittenish pout forms on her lips—the adorable expression shooting an arrow of tenderness straight through my heart. "I can take it. You don't need to coddle me."

"That may be, but we're going to do things my way today, and I say no to the nipple clamps. Now, are you recovered enough for another round or do you need more time?"

"You're one to talk. I'm not the one nearing my forties." A brow of challenge rises as she rolls over and wiggles her ass in a come-hither movement like a cat in heat. "Perhaps I should question your recovery time..." The sexual taunting forces a drop of precum from my dick, dampening my unbuttoned jeans.

"Go ahead, I have no problem proving my stamina." Smacking the round temptation before me, she yelps in dismay, tossing her head and glaring at me. Shrugging, knowing she deserved the light spanking, I get up and shuck the jeans, directing her to the correct position. "On your knees. Hands on top of the headboard."

Crawling forward with hips swaying, Emery obeys, and I fist my heavy cock. Dark curls dance upon her back—begging me to twist the strands around my hand and pull as I ride her hard. Running a knuckle down her spine, I ask, "Where are we on birth control, baby? I'm clean, but I have a condom in my wallet."

"I'm on the pill and clean, too, so we're good. I don't want anything between us."

Perfect.

"Me neither." Squeezing her smaller hands on the wooden headboard, I breathe in the scent of her shampoo, whispering, "Do you remember what I want you to do?"

"Yes..."

"Tell me."

Her voice lowers like she's not used to speaking so bluntly during sex. "Play with my... tits."

"Good girl. Now, show me."

Hesitantly, she reaches up to cup her full breasts, and just like I imagined, her delicate hands barely contain the plump orbs. The tips are already firm and rosy from our earlier play, ready for her touch. Brushing her thumbs back and forth over the sensitive flesh, I begin working my cock between her legs, sliding down through the curls protecting her sex until the mushroom head barely stretches her clenching opening.

"Spread a little wider, baby." She listens immediately, widening her stance awkwardly while continuing to follow my instructions. "You're so wet. I can smell the arousal coating your cunt and thighs, still taste you on my tongue. You're eager for me, aren't you?"

"God, yes!" Her ass pushes back, trying to force my cock deeper inside her pussy. Following through on my fantasy, my hand takes a firm grip on her hair, winding it around my palm, until her head arches back, a soft moan of need escaping her parted lips.

"I'm going to love you so well, Emery. Fuck this pussy so long and hard, you won't be able to walk tomorrow. Everyone at MerryCon will know you've been ridden rough by your man. By me. You want that, don't you? Want them to know while they're fawning over Calder Mayfield or some other guy, you've taken my cock as deep as it can go, felt my seed drip down your thighs."

The more I speak, the hotter I become. Feverish. I need to make her mine. Completely.

Plunging forward without warning, I force Emery to take all of me at once, no niceties, no slow incremental thrusts. Just pure, primal domination.

We both cry out at the sensation of finally being fully connected. And as I set a brutal pace, I watch as she pinches and tugs her nipples, adding to her own pleasure.

One of my hands stabilizes her hips as I rock against her again and again, burying myself deep. "Fuck, you're doing so well, baby, holding me tight, giving yourself to me. Do you feel it, Emery? Feel your claim on me as my cock can't get enough? It'll never be enough."

She moans, incapable of replying, but her hands squeeze her tits firmly, caught up in my words. Her pussy walls contract, and I know she's nearing the breaking point.

"Go ahead, come on my dick, sweetheart. I'll just keep going, desperate to stay in your heat until you drag me into bliss with your next orgasm. Then, I'll suck your sore nipples, soothing them after your harsh treatment. Don't you want that? Want my mouth lapping against your—"

A hoarse cry cuts me off as Emery shudders in pleasure. Sweat slickens the glide of our bodies while I pin her to the headboard, driving my hips into her backside, fucking her through the climax. Doing exactly as I promised.

Long minutes later, I finally relinquish control and allow us both to come, expiring from the intense pleasure. Our heavy breaths dominate the room, and rational thought is slow to return.

Holy fucking hell.

I've never experienced this magnitude of feeling before. From our intimate talks to the mind-blowing sex, Emery is lodged deep in my heart and mind. And what should be terrifying is only mildly alarming. I'll make this work.

I have to.

CHAPTER ELEVEN

EMERY

Morning sunlight wakes me from a dead sleep. I don't think I've ever slept so well in my life, and it's all due to Thatcher. Thinking of him, a kindling of fire reignites in my belly. The things we did. How I let him talk to me, command me. The ache in my muscles reminds me that it was worth it, though, because the man knows his way around a woman and was intent on pleasing me in every way possible.

Ten points for dating an older man.

Smiling at the memory, one hand searches the bed for him but comes up empty. He mentioned after our last round of sex that he'd have to leave early to get to his hotel in time to shower and change for the third day of MerryCon, but I'd hoped to catch him before he left. Sitting up, I realize he tucked the covers around me after getting up, and the sweet gesture brings a giddy grin to my face. Tender and gentle. Rough and demanding. The paradox of Thatcher North.

A folded note falls from his pillow, snagging my attention.

E.

I'm sorry I can't be here when you wake up. Breakfast in bed with your thighs braced on my shoulders, my mouth feasting on your pussy would've been the best way to start the day. Guess we have something to look forward to.

I'll see you later!

Yours,

T.

Collapsing back on my pillow, a glow of light illuminates the sheet of paper as I reread it—each time getting hotter and wetter, envisioning the scene he painted. And soon my hand sneaks under the comforter to feel the resulting arousal.

Setting the note aside, my eyes close as one hand circles my clit and the other flicks over my nipples. They're sore and swollen after last night, but I don't care. Thatcher got me hot and bothered, and the slight pain heightens my pleasure as I pretend the fingers burrowing into my pussy is his cock. So thick like a steel rod. Slamming into me over and over again. "Yes…" I hiss, turned on by the sound of my own pleasure.

Then inspiration strikes.

Pausing for a moment, I grab my phone from the nightstand next to me and contemplate the wisdom of doing what I want to do. Should I send a video? No, anyone could see. A recording? The thought of him listening privately to the melody of my masturbation is too good of an opportunity to pass up.

I've never done something like this. Never even had the idea.

But Thatcher's proven he likes it dirty, and I'm finding so am I. Hallmark, Lifetime, and HAC may provide the sweet, wholesome entertainment I love, but I also enjoyed watching *365 Days*.

Shoring up my courage, I navigate to the recording app on my phone and hit play before resting it on my belly, praying he can hear the wet sucking of fingers in my pussy along with my heavy breathing. Returning to my previous motions, I restart my thrusting, curling my hand to reach my G-spot like he did last night.

"Mmm... Thatch... harder, please." I increase the speed and tug on my nipples, elongating the engorged tips before letting them snap back. A picture of Thatcher listening to me call his name in the throes of a private self-care session forms in my mind, and the fierce look of need I know he'll have spurs me on to turn things up a notch.

My vibrator lays nestled in the drawer next to me, and it's easy enough to grab the eight inch sex toy. Holding it with slippery fingers, I slowly insert it before switching to my favorite vibration setting—the unmistakable buzz ringing loud and clear.

No way he resists touching himself for relief after this.

Plunging the pink toy as far as it can go, the butterfly at the base flutters against my clit, and damp sweat slides down my forehead at the bombardment of sensations. "Thatcher, please. I need you." Another moan rumbles in my throat. "You're so thick, filling me up with your cock."

Minutes later, awareness coalesces in my clit to the point of pain until from one second to the next the pent up energy explodes in sparks of pulsing pleasure. Black dots float in my vision, and my chest heaves from the exertion. *Damn.* That's the best orgasm I've ever given myself. Another thing to thank Thatcher for.

Speaking of...

After struggling to the bathroom where I clean up, I grope for the phone lost on my bed and hit "Stop", then before sanity returns, I hit "Send".

Done.

We'll see what he thinks of that when I arrive at MerryCon today.

CHAPTER TWELVE

THATCHER

She's in for the spanking of her life.

Right after I fuck her until she's hoarse from screaming my name.

The voice note Emery messaged me beckons from its place in my pocket. When I first listened to it, I'd been about to leave for MerryCon, instead I unzipped my slacks and took my cock in hand for a quick release. The fact that she felt bold enough—secure enough—to send a sexy recording of her getting off while thinking of me? It's proof that she's mine.

Whatever comes of this weekend career-wise, I'm not leaving Emery. We'll work through logistics, but she's it for me—no turning back. Leon won't be thrilled, I'm sure, preferring my focus to be solely on the comeback, but if he can't get on-board, then I'll find someone who will. Or give up acting professionally.

I can do theater and keep doing consulting work for a living like I've been doing for the past ten years. Nothing's off-limits when it comes to keeping Emery for my own. And the notion strikes me as a stark contrast from my feelings before MerryCon. When fear gripped my chest at the possibility of no fans and messing up my second chance, but a calmness has settled over me since Emery. If I have her, my life will be better—whether I'm acting professionally again or not.

Entering the large area of booths, there's a determined pep in my stride as I head towards the table I've shared with Emery for the past two days. But when I near our spot, she's chatting with Calder Mayfield, laughing with him, and his hand caresses her arm.

Red colors my field of vision. What the fuck?

Emery's flustered babble when describing Calder as her top wish of MerryCon and their flirty banter from the stocking contest replays in my head. Could she still want Calder? Does she think since she nabbed me, she can seduce another actor?

The ugly queries clog any rational thinking. And they call forth all the horrible reviews I received after *The Headley's* ended, reminding me of what a failure I used to be.

Still am.

Pain stabs in the vicinity of my heart, and a cruel streak makes me want to hurt her the same way.

No, that's your insecurity talking.

Fists clench in my coat pockets as bullish breaths expel from my nose.

This is Emery. Sweet, kind Emery. Who gave herself to you last night. Made love to you until the early hours of today. She wouldn't betray you. She's just being her friendly self towards a celebrity whose work she enjoys. That's all.

The brief pep talk propels me forward, intent on discovering for myself what Emery is feeling. I don't like being this vulnerable, and it's not something I accounted for with our relationship. *Stupid.*

"Good morning." I offer a hand of greeting to Calder, gaze shifting to Emery and taking rapid inventory. There's a red mark on her neck from one of the many love bites I gave her, the scarf she's wearing to hide it dipping below the minor bruise. And she's in another thin bra that fails to disguise her assets through the tee shirt. I check to see if Calder notices, but his attention remains neutral and upward.

"Thatch, how's it going? Today promises to be fun with a gingerbread house making contest. Maybe you'll place this time." He gives me a good-natured punch to the shoulder before someone in his entourage waves him over.

Saying good-bye, Emery and I are left standing alone except for the milling crowd around us. "I missed you this morning," Emery says, smiling and stepping closer.

All at once, the ridiculousness of my jealousy seems obvious, and embarrassment at the immature reaction seeps into my bones. "Me, too. Although you tried to remedy the situation with quite an enlightening recording."

"Did you like it then?" Vulnerability edges her irises as if I could have anything negative to say about the gift she gave me.

"I loved it." *And you.*

Wait, what?

Love isn't right. I'll admit to falling for her and definitely claiming her. But being in love? This isn't one of my movies. It can't happen in real life... Can it?

"I'm glad because I worked very hard on producing a satisfactory product." She winks and skips a little to our table, preparing for another long day of waiting for fans to get their pictures taken with me.

"Hmm... such a busy little elf. One would think that would put you on Santa's nice list, but we both know you're as naughty as they come." Settling into the seat next to hers, my hand slips under the tablecloth to squeeze her thigh.

"Perhaps, But it's only because you've corrupted me."

A jovial laugh bursts forth. "I haven't had enough time to corrupt you. Don't blame me for your mischievous streak... So, what were you and Calder discussing?" The question pops out before I can stop it.

"Oh, he stopped by to wish us luck during the gingerbread contest today, said he was bringing his A-game since he filmed a storyline centering around gingerbread houses."

"Of course, he did." If only my holiday movie about saving a family-owned antique shop would come in handy.

"I'm not intimidated; we've got this." She reassures me with a pat on my hand, and I turn it over to capture hers.

"Yeah, we do..." Clearing my throat, I broach the topic of after MerryCon while it's still quiet in our non-existent line. "Emery. How would you feel about continuing our relationship past this weekend? To be honest, I already care a great deal for you and don't want this to be a four-day fling."

"You don't?"

"No. I've been stuck for the past decade, flopping again and again. I thought jump starting my career would fix the feeling, but it hasn't. And I know I'm still in the early stages, but even if I became Hollywood's hottest item tomorrow, I don't think that sense of being in a rut would go away." Pouring my heart out to her. Sharing the secret I hadn't told anyone feels like the most natural thing in the world. "But with you... I feel like I know where I'm going again, like I have purpose and can move forward with my life. You breezed in here for a short holiday gig, but you ended up turning my world upside down."

"Oh, Thatcher." Glancing around the building, Emery shakes her head in frustration. "I wish we were alone for this conversation."

"Sorry, I could've warned you I have terrible timing." I shrug sheepishly. It's a flaw that's plagued me all my life.

"Nevertheless, this needs to be said." She faces me fully, an earnest expression brightening her eyes. "Call it the magic of Christmas or the magic of these movies, but you described exactly what's happening in my own heart. And it's not some fantasy I'm overhyping because I loved your films or have had a crush on you forever like it was with Calder. You're real to me. A flesh and blood man who's more than what you do for a living." A well of tears glimmer in her eyes until she blinks them away with a self-conscious chuckle. "Ugh, I do not want to cry during this... Thatcher, you see me. You say you care for me, and I trust that you do because you show it in your actions. It's just who you are. I'm not sure what comes next for us, but if you're willing, then so am I. I want to take the next step with you."

Unrepentant joy warms me from head to toe. Emery wants me. Thatcher North, the man—not the childhood actor or the failed actor or the older, comeback actor—just me as I am.

"This may not be the smartest decision, but I can't hear you say those things and sit here and behave. I've got to kiss you." Wrapping a hand around her neck, I tug her towards me until our mouths meet to seal the promise we made each other. To try to make this work. To be together.

"Awww..." Clicks from cameras go off in a flash along with a few happy claps, but let them cheer and watch. Because Christmas came early this year, and I couldn't have asked for a better gift.

EPILOGUE ONE

EMERY
ONE YEAR LATER

C hristmas music swells in the arena as the fifth year of MerryCon continues. It's strange being back again—married to the man I was assigned to help last year. As Thatcher's wife, I've met a bevy of my favorite Hallmark, Lifetime, & HAC stars, some who've become really good friends. However, the best perk of being married is having Thatcher as a husband.

Attentive and devoted, he's the dream man I feared would never materialize, who only existed in movies. But he definitely exists and loves me unconditionally.

The first few months of our relationship had its share of road bumps until I was able to join him on the road. Our lives consisted of auditions and booked projects, something we were all extremely grateful for, especially his manager Leon.

"What are you thinking about?" Thatcher kisses me on the forehead, drawing my attention as we enjoy a few spare minutes away from the crowd.

"Just everything that's changed since we were here."

"Are you happy with the changes? Travelling so much can be a lot." It's a conversation we've had numerous times as he always checks in to gauge my feelings, willing to slow down if I ever have enough. Another reason I love him.

"It's been an adventure, and I wouldn't go back to my old life for all the hot cocoa in the world!" I joke, lifting a snowman mug brimming with the chocolatey goodness.

A grunt of amusement vibrates in his throat before he tugs on a loose curl draped over my shoulder. "Same... Though maybe for all the snickerdoodles..."

"Hey! I'm better than a cookie!" After learning his fondness for snickerdoodles, it's become a tradition to bake a batch every Sunday for us to share while watching a movie. He always points out how my brown sugar and cinnamon scent was one of the first things he noticed about me—after appreciating my curves, of course.

One of these days I should send a thank-you note to the store where I bought the brown sugar and cinnamon lotion that captured his attention. It sent me down a course I never could've imagined for myself.

Married to an older leading man—someone I overlooked in the past—yet now know is the perfect man for me.

EPILOGUE TWO

THATCHER
THREE YEARS LATER

"**A**nd that's a wrap! Thank you everybody for your hard work." The director starts a round of applause as the cast and crew celebrate the ending of another Christmas film. It's my final one for the season and eighth movie this year. A prayer of thanks goes up at my good fortune.

After the success of MerryCon and the support of Emery, my comeback became a reality as I landed role after role, becoming a mainstay in HAC's lineup of stars. I'd learned from my youthful mistakes and finally had the career I'd always dreamed of as a kid.

But my true victory was Emery. Making her my wife.

Driving to the hotel we're staying at for filming, I race to get back to her, never quite losing the obsession to have her near. If anything, it's only increased in depth. Loving someone fiercely and receiving that love just as strongly is an experience I can't describe. I've been happier than I've ever been, and despite the arguments we may have, the love doesn't diminish.

Twenty minutes later, the room is empty when I step inside. *Where's Emery?*

Then a wave of steam spills into the air as the bathroom door opens, and she walks out barefoot, wrapped only in a white towel. Instantly, I want her. Thirsty for the drops of water sliding down her skin.

"You're back already. I thought you might be a few hours more." She tugs a brush through her wet hair, pulling harshly at tangles.

"Everyone figured we'd wrap today, so we did our best work to finish early. Come here." A finger crooks to motion her over.

Emery's arm suspends its movement until she tosses the brush to a nightstand. "I recognize that look. I just got clean, now you want to dirty me up again?"

"Damn straight. Get your curvy little body over here, wife."

Sauntering forward, she stops just out of reach. "As you wish, *husband*, but there's something I want to do before you go all caveman on me. It's a sort of reward for finishing another project."

"Hmm... sounds intriguing. Though, I can't guarantee the caveman thing, but I'm willing to try. What do you have in mind?"

Choosing a pillow from the top of the bed, Emery drops it to the ground before kneeling. Impish blue eyes glitter up at me as she separates the edges of her towel—the languid pace teasing me until her naked curves are revealed.

"I thought of you in the shower just now." She begins, unbuckling my belt and parting my jeans. "There's a detachable spout in there, and I was feeling a little achy. Hoped a quick release might help. So, I let the warm water splash against my clit, all the while my mouth felt empty. I wanted to suck you off. Needed to feel your pleasure, as well."

"Well, I'm at your disposal, sweetheart." The guttural tone in my voice is unrecognizable, garbling the words in my suddenly dry mouth.

"Aren't you always?" A twinkle of laughter sparkles in her gaze before darkening in desire. My cock's in her hand now, stiff and throbbing—greedy for her mouth. "I used to think I wouldn't like this very much. Have I ever told you that?"

A tremble of need slithers over my nerves as I shake my head in a negative reply. "No?" She licks precum off the tip. "Probably because it didn't matter once I met you." Light kisses trail down the heated skin, coasting along a raised vein. "You call to the seductress in me. The woman whose only desire is to please her lover anyway she can."

"It's only fair considering the filthy Neanderthal traits you expose in me."

"Mmm... yes, you do become a bit untamed at times." Emery's lips circle the mushroom head and suckle, lashes lifting, daring me to watch the hollowing of her cheeks as she takes me deeper before sliding back. It's a leisurely speed meant to torture me. But hell if I care.

This is about more than physical satisfaction. This is Emery loving me, showing her adoration while wielding the power she holds over me.

Tangling my hands in damp curls, I don't force her to quicken the pace but massage her scalp, eliciting a moan of bliss. Two can play this game—because she's my life.

The woman I want by my side for the next fifty years.

The volunteer turned lover turned wife.

And Christmas made it all happen.

Curious about Calder Mayfield?

His story will be available December 2023!
Until then, keep the cozy vibes alive with a trip to the mountains of the
Lumberjacks of High Ridge series...

Kept by the Beast

All Poppy wanted was a relaxing trip to the cute mountain town of High
Ridge. She didn't plan on getting stranded with no one to call for help. What's a
shy, curvy girl to do?

Asa is known as the town's Beast. Large and foreboding, women run in fear
and revulsion. But when this mountain man happens upon a curvy damsel in
distress, could she be the one woman to accept him for who he is?

*Two virgins stranded in a cabin...Things are heating up on the mountain
when a curvy girl meets this beastly lumberjack in a steamy story of
insta-love!*

THANKS FOR READING & DON'T FORGET TO RATE/ REVIEW!

Please consider leaving a rating/review on Amazon, Goodreads, Instagram, TikTok, and/or any other sites you review on. Ratings & reviews are the #1 way to support an indie author like me.

They don't have to be long or even positive (though I hope you enjoyed this book!). All the algorithms care about are QUANTITY.

The more reviews, the more my books are shown to other potential readers!

And they serve as guides to readers on whether or not to take a chance on an indie author.

Also, don't miss out on free books and up-to-date release information. You can sign up for my newsletter here.

I appreciate your support!

XO, Hallie

ABOUT THE AUTHOR

Hallie prefers steamy, insta-love stories where curvy girls are claimed by filthy-talking heroes. And when she ran out of reading material, she decided to write her own stories. If you want a quick, hot read, she's your girl!